TURTLE IN PARADISE
The Graphic Novel

ALSO BY JENNIFER L. HOLM

Boston Jane: An Adventure
Boston Jane: Wilderness Days
Boston Jane: The Claim
The Fourteenth Goldfish
The Third Mushroom
The Lion of Mars
Middle School Is Worse Than Meatloaf
Eighth Grade Is Making Me Sick
Our Only May Amelia
Penny from Heaven
Turtle in Paradise
Full of Beans

BY JENNIFER L. HOLM AND MATTHEW HOLM

Sunny Side Up
Swing It, Sunny
Sunny Rolls the Dice
The Babymouse series
The Evil Princess vs. the Brave Knight series
The Squish series
My First Comics series

ALSO BY SAVANNA GANUCHEAU

Bloom (with Kevin Panetta)

JENNIFER L. HOLM AND SAVANNA GANUCHEAU

COLORS BY LARK PIEN

Photo credits: p. 235: © Bettmann/CORBIS. p. 236: Library of Congress, Prints and Photographs Division, FSA/OWI Collection, LC-USF34-026281-PDLC. p. 237 (top): Monroe County Library. p. 237 (bottom): Personal collection of Cathy Porter, used by permission. p. 238: State Archives of Florida.

Visit us on the web and sign up for our newsletter! RHKidsGraphic.com • @RHKidsGraphic

Educators and librarians, for a variety of teaching tools, visit us at RHTeachersLibrarians.com

Library of Congress Cataloging-in-Publication Data is available upon request.
ISBN 978-0-593-12630-1 (pbk) — ISBN 978-0-593-12631-8 (trade) —
ISBN 978-0-593-12632-5 (library binding) — ISBN 978-0-593-12633-2 (ebook)

Designed by Patrick Crotty

MANUFACTURED IN CHINA
10 9 8 7 6 5 4 3 2 1
First Edition

A comic on every bookshelf.

Turtle in Paradise was drawn and colored digitally in Photoshop. It was lettered using the font Smiling Cat.

For my Conch cuzzies, Kurt and Monica —J.H.

Conch

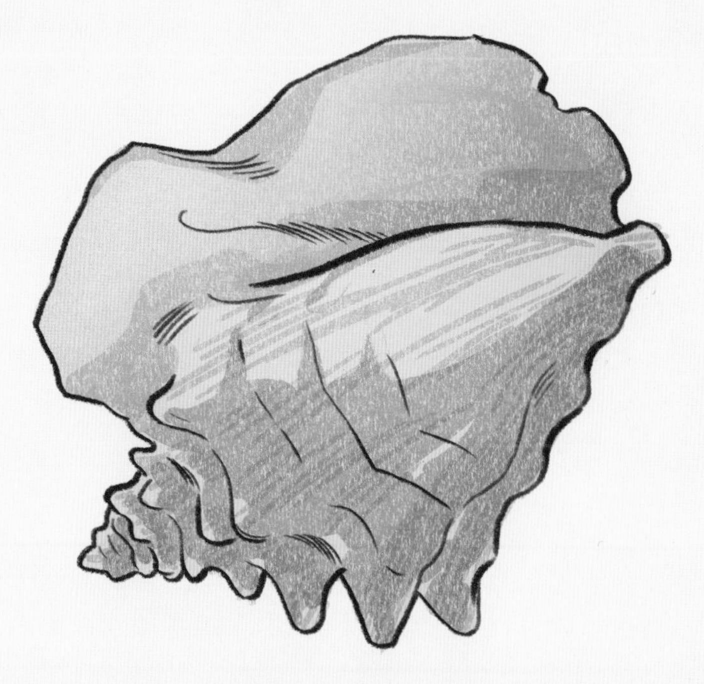

Pronunciation: 'känk, 'känch
Function: noun
1: any of various large spiral-shelled marine gastropod mollusks (as of the genus *Strombus*)
2: often capitalized: a native or resident of the Florida Keys

—*Merriam-Webster's Collegiate Dictionary*, 11th edition

Rotten Kids

June 1935
VVVVe
BMP

Everyone thinks children are sweet as Necco Wafers.
Blehh
But I've lived long enough to know the truth.

Kids are rotten.
hmph
What do you think of my new hair, Turtle?
It sure is coming in thick, Mr. Edgit.
I tell you, Turtle, Hair Today is the best product on the market!
HAIR TODAY
HAIR TODAY
I'm going to sell buckets of the stuff. It really makes your hair grow, I tell yah! Got my own testimonial right here on my head.
I'm gonna be rich like Daddy Warbucks— just you wait and see!
Now, the only way Mr. Edgit is going to sell a million is if he got Archie on the case. Archie could sell a trap to a mouse.

KNOCK
KNOCK
Well, hello, sweet thing. Is the lady of the house at home?
I'm not sweet. I slugged Ronald Carruthers when he tried to throw my cat in the well, and I'd do it again.

HA
HA
HA
Housewives can't resist him.
Who's at the door, Turtle?
Some sales fella.
I know Mama couldn't.
Nice to meet you, ma'am. My name's Archie.
Mama put her hand over her heart, and it was a good thing, too.
Otherwise, it would have jumped right out of her chest.

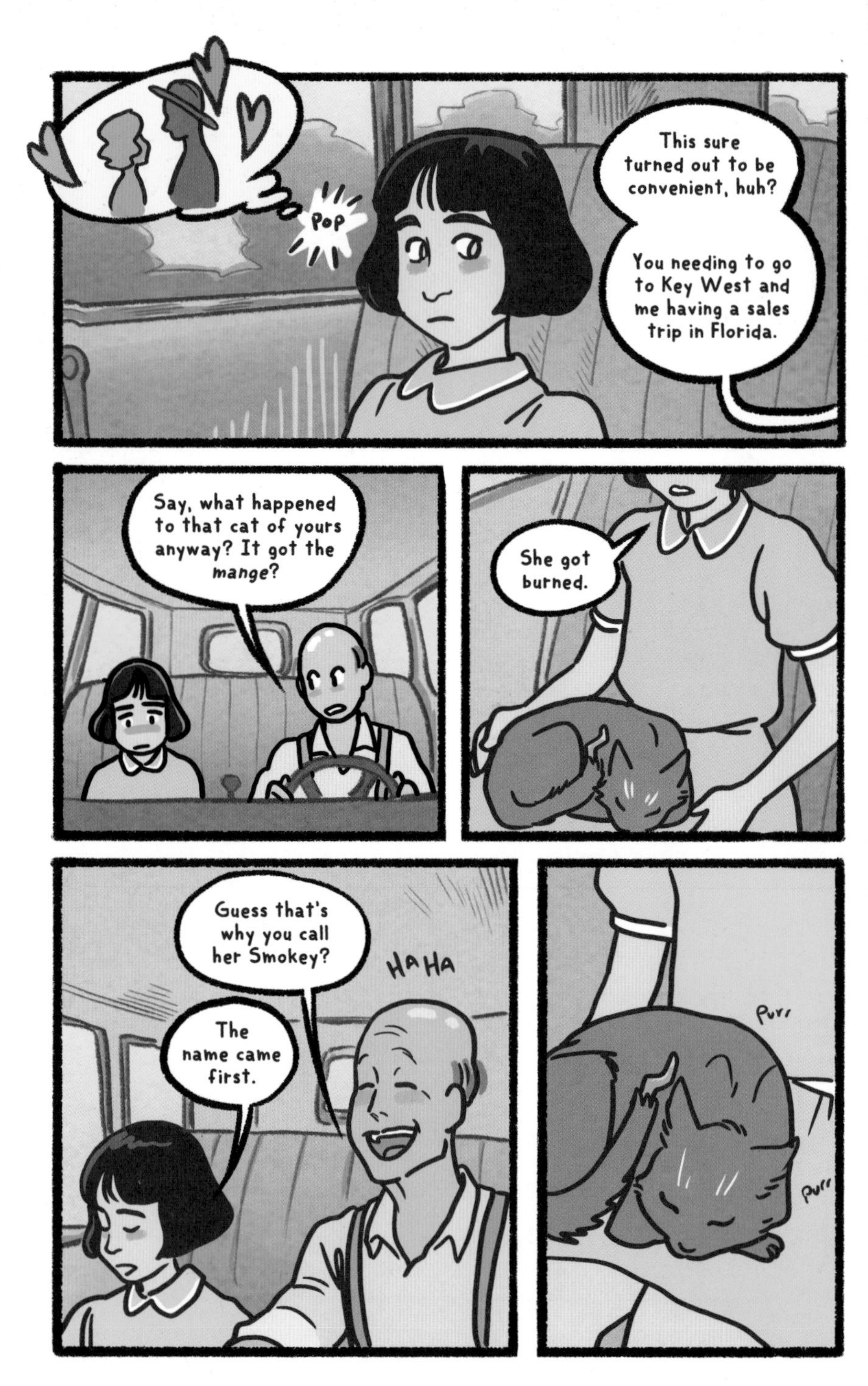
POP
This sure turned out to be convenient, huh?
You needing to go to Key West and me having a sales trip in Florida.
Say, what happened to that cat of yours anyway? It got the *mange*?
She got burned.
Guess that's why you call her Smokey?
HAHA
The name came first.
Purr
Purr

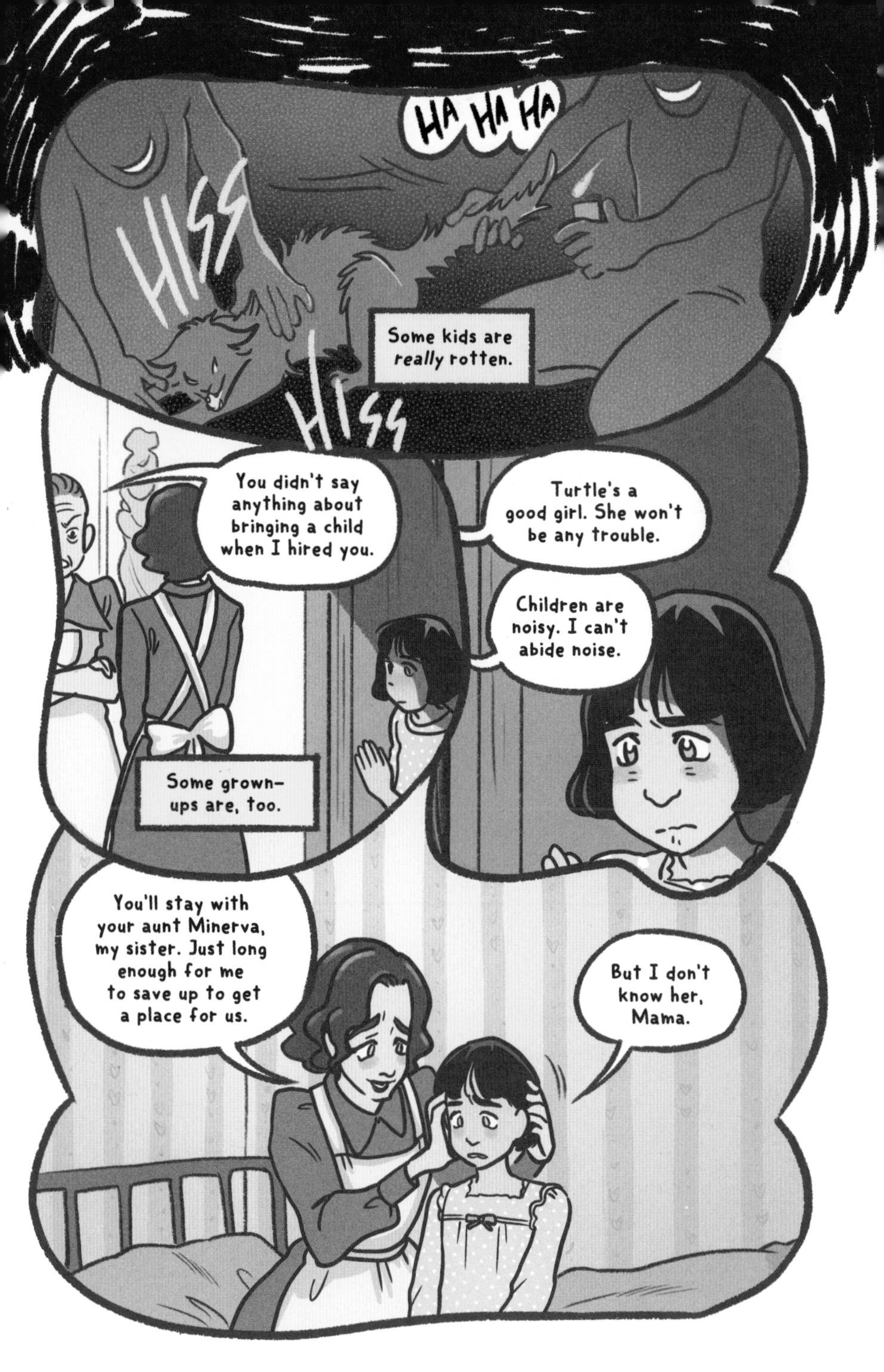
HA HA HA
HISS
Some kids are *really* rotten.
HISS
You didn't say anything about bringing a child when I hired you.
Turtle's a good girl. She won't be any trouble.
Children are noisy. I can't abide noise.
Some grown-ups are, too.
You'll stay with your aunt Minerva, my sister. Just long enough for me to save up to get a place for us.
But I don't know her, Mama.

Minnie's happy to have you stay with her, and you'll *love* Key West, baby.
It's paradise.
And someday, we'll have our own house.
The Bellewood.
Won't that be swell?
The Bellewood
The Cedars
Yes, Mama.
Mama's like that.

She's always had stars in her eyes.
BMP
She believes in Hollywood endings.
Not me.
VRROOM

Paradise Lost

Well, we finally made it. So this is Key West, huh? Sure took forever and a day to get here.

What a dump.
I can't tell where this "Curry Lane" is.
These people ever hear of street signs?
Hey, kid! Can you tell me where Curry Lane is?

Which one's the Currys' place?
You're looking at it.
BOOF
They're all Currys', mister. It's Curry Lane.
Come on, Turtle. At least we're in the right place.
WILL WURK FOR CANDY
So what are you selling, mister?
Well, since you asked, I do happen to have some Hair Today back in my automobile!
ROW
ROWF

What's it do?
Makes your hair grow!
ROW
ROWF
ROW
Guess you ain't a satisfied customer.
ROF
ROW ROW
HA HA HAAAA!!!
ROF ROW ROWF
Smokey's never been scared of dogs. Just kids.

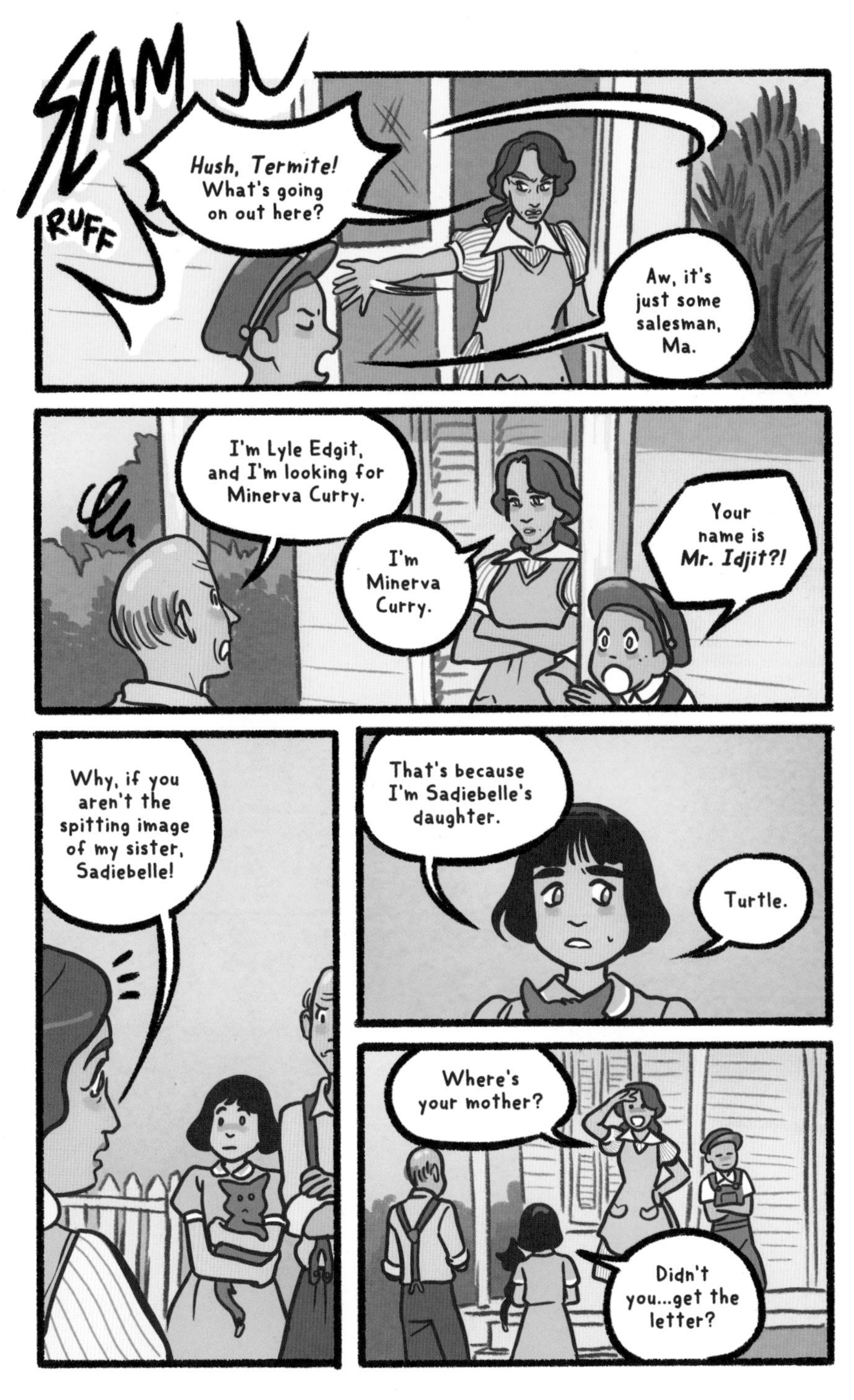
SLAM
RUFF
Hush, Termite! What's going on out here?
Aw, it's just some salesman, Ma.
I'm Lyle Edgit, and I'm looking for Minerva Curry.
I'm Minerva Curry.
Your name is Mr. Idjit?!
Why, if you aren't the spitting image of my sister, Sadiebelle!
That's because I'm Sadiebelle's daughter.
Turtle.
Where's your mother?
Didn't you...get the letter?

What letter?
Did something happen to her?
Mama got a new job as a housekeeper, and Mrs. Budnick doesn't like children so she sent me from New Jersey to live with you...
This is just like Sadiebelle. She never thinks.
sigh
As if I don't have enough already with three kids and a husband who's never home.
Well, Turtle...
PAT
I'll leave you to your happy family reunion.

See ya, Mr. *Idjit*!
Ma! I had an accident!
Ma, Buddy's calling.
Beans, help your cousin with her bag.
Let me help you with your bag, *Tortoise*.
!
TOSS
HA HA HA HA

It's Turtle.

Lucky as an Orphan

I used to feel sorry for orphans...
...but Little Orphan Annie got adopted by Daddy Warbucks...
CREAK
That's just about as lucky as it gets.
I bet she doesn't have to worry about being sent to a house that's tiny and dark and smells like sour milk.

Where should I put my suitcase?
The boys will have to share, I suppose. You can stay in Beans's room. Upstairs to the left.

Is that your cat?
Hop
That's Smokey.
What happened to him?
Some boys lit her tail on fire.

Beans, did you take my shooter? If you fed another marble to the gulls, I'll tell Ma.
Who're you?!
What's the big idea?
I'm Buddy!
For Pete's sake, Buddy, go put some pants on! Kermit, get back to your nap right now! Beans, your cousin is staying in your room.
But, Ma!
ROFF
ROWF
Beans, get Termite out of here.
Ma! I ain't tired, and Beans ain't sleeping with us, no way no how!
Why can't she stay with the little pests?
ROW ROW
Smokey can sleep with me!

Why should Termite go?! He was here first!
I don't have to take a nap. I'm four!
Ma! Please! I don't wanna sleep!
ROWF
ROWF
ROWF
ROWF
ROWF
THAT'S IT!
YOU KIDS GET OUT OF THIS HOUSE!

PUSH
Don't come back inside until I say so!
...
Well, that's one way out of a nap.
Aren't you a little old for naps?
I had rheumatic fever, and now I've got a weak heart.
Hey, fellas!
Kermit almost died!

Hey,
Pork Chop!
Pork Chop?
Pork Chop and Beans. They just go together.
Who's she?
Aw, some freeloading cousin from New Jersey.
Well, if it ain't the Diaper Gang.
Hi, Jelly!

Mr. Gardner delivered it to me by mistake.
JUNE 7 1935 FLORIDA
Minerva Curry
Curry Lane
Key West, Florida
U S A
Must be for you, *Tortoise.*
Diaper Gang's got itself a new member, I see.
You mean her? She's not in the gang. No girls *allowed.*
You got a club called the Diaper Gang? What do you do? Change diapers?
Course we change diapers!
We watch babies. Bad babies. The crying kind.
We get paid in candy!

And there's rules.
First rule of the Diaper Gang is you gotta know the rules.
Oooh! Oooh!
I know the rules!
Then it's no girls allowed,
keep your rag clean,
always duck,
and...
...never tell anyone the secret formula.
Secret formula?
For diaper rash.
Cures it like that.
SNAP

Hey, Beans. You think it'll work on this? Nicked myself shaving.
Works on everything, Jelly, but it'll cost you.
But I'm your cousin!
Sorry, Jelly. Business is business.
You're pretty hard for an eleven-year-old, Beans.
Gotta be to handle bad babies.
You ever take care of good babies?
Ain't no such thing.
That's why we're always in business.

The Conch Telegraph

clink
What is it?
Alligator pear on Cuban bread.
I don't cater to fussy children.
...
CHOMP

I read the letter from your mother...She says she's planning on marrying this Archie fella. He planning on marrying her?
I don't know.
What's he do?
He's a salesman.
Is he nice? Is he good to her?
TAP
He bought me these shoes.
I spent my whole childhood taking care of Sadiebelle, and here I am taking care of you now. I sure hope you have more sense than her.
What's an alligator pear anyhow?
HA!
Are all kids from New Jersey as dumb as you?

That's an alligator pear.
What does this Archie sell, anyway?
That's an avocado...
Encyclopedias.
Encyclopedias? To who?
Dumb kids like you who don't know what an avocado is.
Ready, pal?
Ready!
Can I come?
Course you can't come, Buddy.
Take Buddy with you. Turtle, too. I don't want children underfoot. I need to finish all this laundry today or Mrs. Cardillo won't pay me.

Vrrr
vrrrr
Where are we going?
We got Pudding today.
WAAAAAAAAAA
KNOCK
KNOCK
WAHHH
Mornin', Mrs. Lowe.
UWAAA
Oh, Beans, I don't think I've ever been so happy to see someone.
AAAAA
How's he doing?

WA AAUWAAAA
I swear he didn't sleep more than five minutes last night! He's teething real bad.
Don't worry, Mrs. Lowe. We'll take care of him.
WAAAAAA
AAAAAA
What's wrong with him?
WAAAAA
Nothing. Pudding's the worst baby we've ever had.
TUCK
AAAA
His mother spoils him. Picks him up every time he cries.
That's why we don't let girls in the gang. Girls always want to pick up babies.
WAAAAAAA

Not me. I'm not picking up any baby.
WAAAAAAA
Time to wrap him up.
UUUUAA
UU WAA UUU AHH!
hic hic
I don't like babies. They're like Shirley Temple: everyone thinks they're cute, but the fact is they're annoying.
WAA— A-JUU MM MAMA ZZZZ
Works every time.
WILL WURK CANDY

ICE
Got any spare chips, Mr. Roberts?
Sure thing, Beans.
You must be Turtle. My, I do believe you are as pretty as your mother.
?
How come everyone knows who I am?
Conch telegraph.
shrug
Conchs like to talk. Everyone knew you were here five minutes after you showed up yesterday.

Mama told me that Conchs were what folks in Key West call themselves. A lot of them originally came from the Bahamas, where they fished for conch.
When I asked Mama about my Conch relatives, she said her parents had been dead for a long time, but that I had a lot of Conch cousins.
Too bad she didn't tell me that they were all snotty boys.

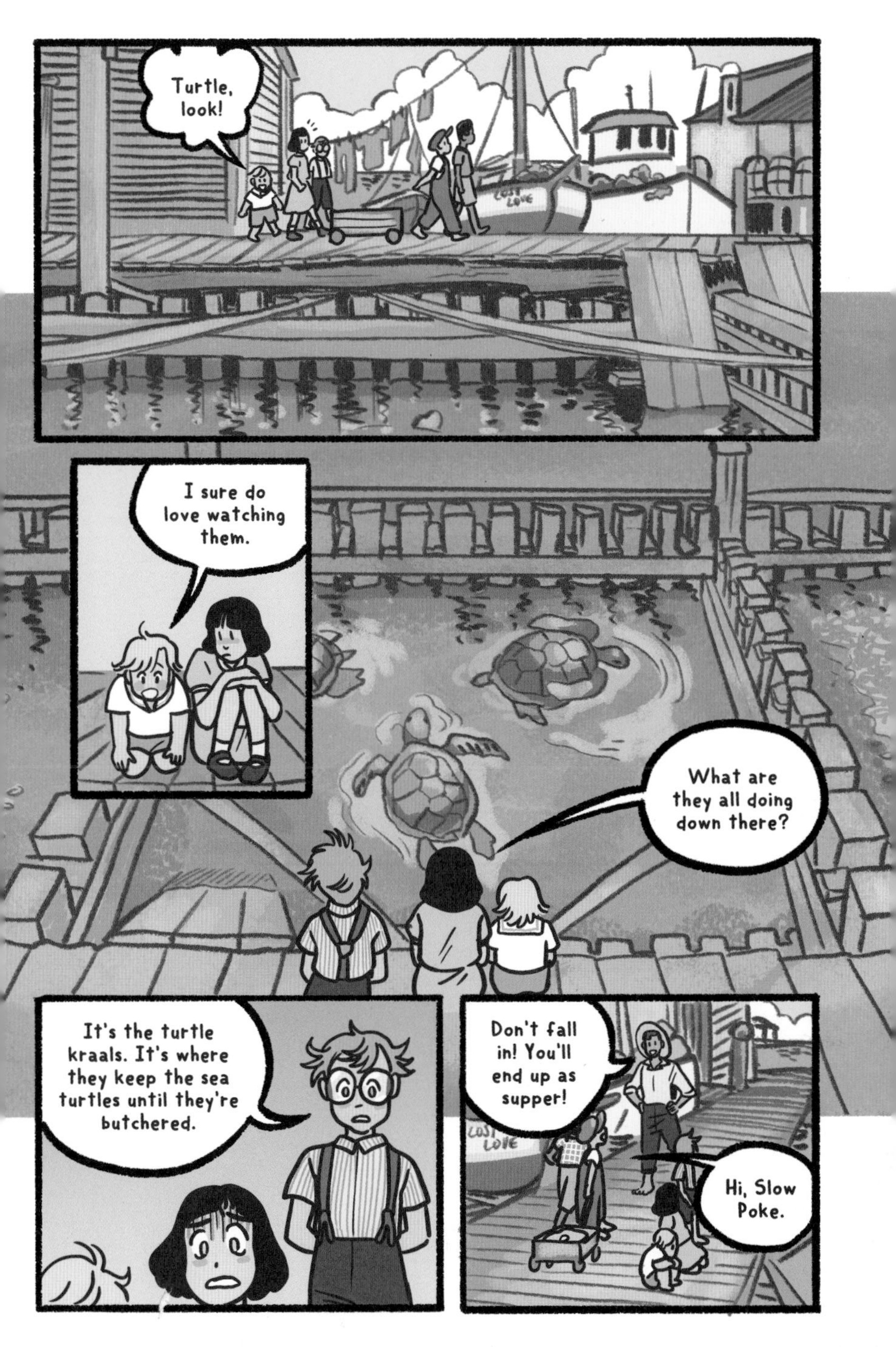
Turtle, look!
I sure do love watching them.
What are they all doing down there?
It's the turtle kraals. It's where they keep the sea turtles until they're butchered.
Don't fall in! You'll end up as supper!
Hi, Slow Poke.

Hey, Beans! I stopped in at Matecumbe and saw your dad. He said to say hi.
GREEN CARNATION
Thanks. I hear you lost your first mate. Why don't you hire me? You know what a good sailor I am.
I know, but I already hired Ollie. I'll be sure to keep you in mind for next time.
Oh! Who's your friend here?
This is Turtle. She's a cousin, and she's got a cat named Smokey.
Oh...

Turtle, huh?
You wouldn't happen to be related to Sadiebelle Gifford?
That's my mama.
Really? Is she here with you?
She's in New Jersey.
I see.
Say, Slow Poke, you get any loggerheads?
Not this time, but I did all right.

The Lost Love
What are those?
They're sponges.
That's gold you're looking at.
Sure don't look like any sponge I've ever seen.
Gotta clean 'em yet. Then they'll be fine enough for a lady's face.
We gotta keep moving, Slow Poke, or Pudding will wake up. He's teething bad.
Maybe try a little whiskey on his gums.
We did once. It didn't work.
Maybe you didn't use enough?
wave

Can You Spare a Nickel, Pal?

The gang's got babies today. Do you want to come along?
Uh...
Buddy! You did *not* just have an accident!
You hang around here and you're gonna end up watching Buddy. Believe me, he's worse than all those babies put together.

We got three today.
Who said she could come?
Just let her come already...
You need help today, Beans?
Nope.
Hey, Beans, you got babies?
Yeah. Yeah.
Beans?
No.
I guess it's the same all over. Everyone just wants a job.

Where's your father?
He's up in Matecumbe, working on the highway.
Ma didn't want to move. She said it's a wilderness up there. Poppy comes home every few weeks.
At least he's got a job.
WAH!
Uh-oh.
UU WAH!
I think Pudding's got a bad diaper.
WAAAAA
WAAAAA

WAAAOOH WAAAAAA
Look at his bungy! No wonder the kid's crying.
AAAAAAA
Bungy?
What? Kids in New Jersey don't have bungys?
Use the formula.
That's the secret diaper formula?
Yep.
What's in it?
?
It's a secret! You've gotta be in the Diaper Gang!
Speaking of wanting to be in the Diaper Gang, look who's coming.

Hey, Beans.
Hey, Too Bad.
I went to the lane, but your mom said you left already.
We've got babies.
See, I was wonderin' if I could have another try.
We've given you three tries already, Too Bad.
But I've been practicing! Honest, I have.

Give him a baby.
heh
WAAAAAAA
UM!
UHH!
WWAAAAAAGH
ACK!
SPRAY
HA HA HA HA
Rule number four, always duck.
UGH!
HA HA HA HA
...

See you later, Too Bad!
Yeah, too bad you'll never be in the Diaper Gang!
Ha
Ha
Ha
Why don't you work for money?

Who'd pay us? Most of the island is on relief.
Here, you can have some of mine.
Hey, that's the Diaper Gang's mango candy!
DING DING DING DING DING
Jimmy.
I want some ice cream!
We ain't got no nickels.
ICE CREAM

Don't need nickels. I've got charm. You watch.
Soursop, Jimmy.
That's a nickel, Beans.
Can you spare me a nickel?
Can't do it, Beans. You still haven't paid me back from last time.
Sorry, Beans, business is business.
Charm only gets you so far. You've gotta have smarts, too...
I'm Turtle.
...and I've got smarts a-plenty.

I'm Jimmy. What can I get you? I've got tamarind, mango, coconut, soursop, and sugar apple.
I'll try the sugar apple.
That's a nickel, young lady.
Oh no! The nickel was in the bottom of the can, Jimmy!
!
In the bottom of the can, you say?
scratch scratch
sigh

I'm going to have to eat my way to it. Might take a while.
Oh, go on! You can only get away with that once, though.
ICE CREAM
Say, you aren't going to eat the whole thing by yourself, are you?
Sorry. Can't share with you. After all, I'm not in the Diaper Gang.

Truth of the Matter

Aunt Minnie doesn't have a phone, but Pudding's mama lets me borrow hers.
Hello?
It's me, Mama.
Oh, baby. I was so worried.
Mama—
Sadiebelle, you know I don't allow the help to use my personal telephone.
Sorry, Mrs. Budnick.
I have to go, baby. I'll write you.

Click
Dooot
Doooot
Doooo
click

Don't you want to play marbles?
Buddy, don't you get to playing and forget to go. I'm tired of washing your pants.
GASP!
Where did you get those paper dolls?
Mama gave them to me for my birthday.
Those are my dolls.
She said they were hers.
Well, she must have forgotten about stealing them from *me*.

You want them back?
Of course I want them back! They're mine, aren't they?
SNATCH
Do I want my dolls back? Pfff!
...
Do you want to play marbles now?

WOO!
GOTCHA!
HAHA
AH!
HAHA
TAG!
KERMIT!

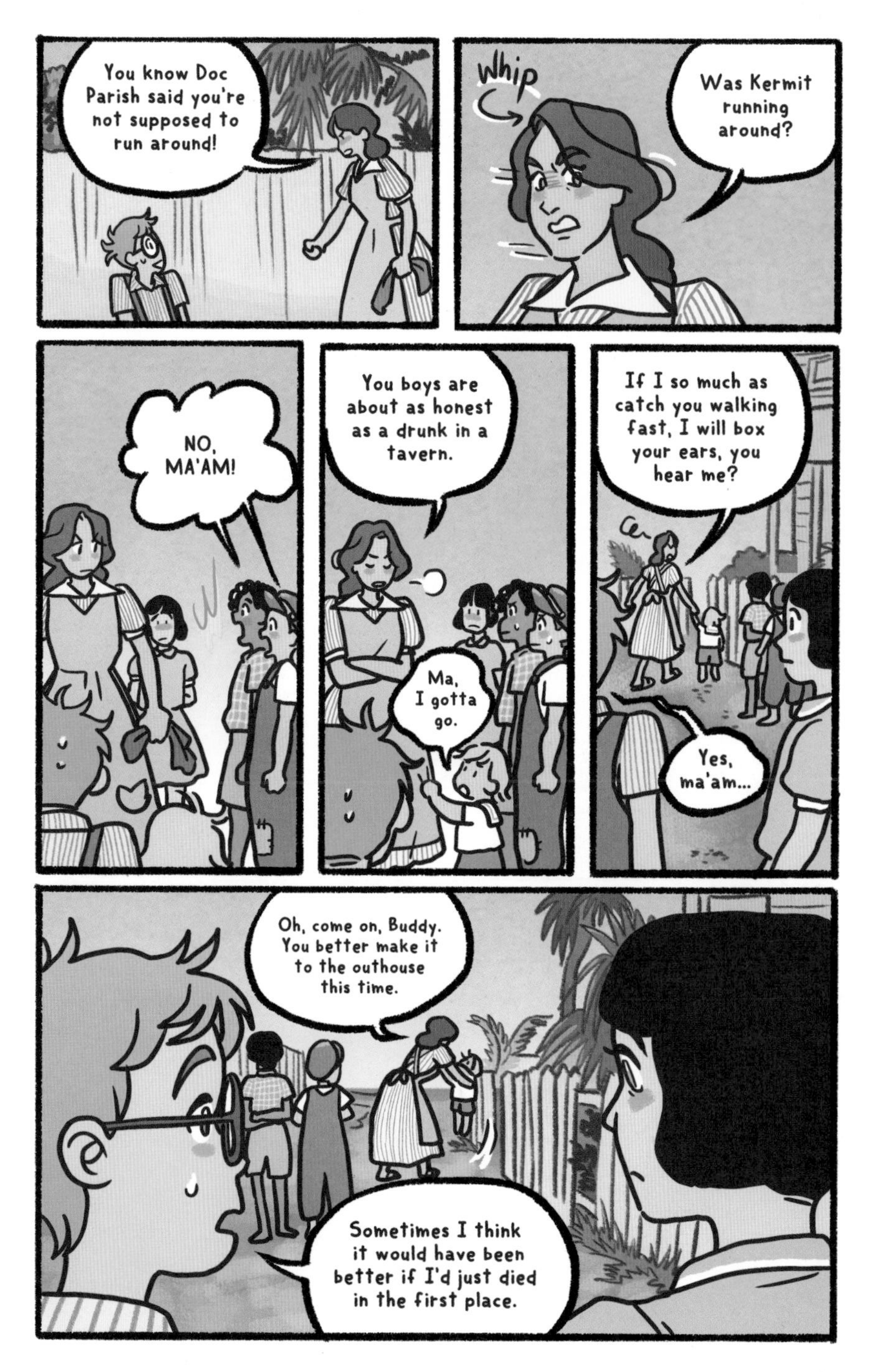
You know Doc Parish said you're not supposed to run around!
Whip
Was Kermit running around?
NO, MA'AM!
You boys are about as honest as a drunk in a tavern.
Ma, I gotta go.
If I so much as catch you walking fast, I will box your ears, you hear me?
Yes, ma'am...
Oh, come on, Buddy. You better make it to the outhouse this time.
Sometimes I think it would have been better if I'd just died in the first place.

TAG!
I'm already it!
You want to go to Duval Street?
All right.
Would your heart really give out from running around?
TURN
?
Huh?
I don't know... Want to find out?
DASH
HA HA HA

Duval Street is like a prettified version of Key West. Kermit tells me that they're trying to get tourists to come down here, which is why it's all fixed up.
PALACE

S.H KRESS & CO.
CENTS
KRESS
There's even a movie theater. Too bad it's showing a Shirley Temple picture.

Kermit knows everyone. He's like the unofficial mayor of Key West.
Hi, Cheap Joe!
Hey, Kitty Gray!
Say, Kermit, you know anywhere I could make some dough?
What for?
So Mama and I can buy a house. The payments are forty-five dollars a month.
Forty-five?!
Let's ask Johnny Cakes! I hear he's always looking for help. He brings rum from the Bahamas. It's illegal.
PEPE'S

There he is!
Hey, Johnny Cakes!
Well, well. If it isn't our Kermit.
And who is this lovely lady?
This is my cousin Turtle.
I hear you have a fast boat.

Fast enough.
You hiring?
I don't normally hire kids.
I don't mind illegal activities.
What do you think I do?!
You're a rumrunner! Just last Saturday, Cousin Dizzy said you brought in a haul of the best rum he's ever tasted.
He's got you there, Johnny!
HA HA
Be careful, Johnny. These two are the sharpest in town.
You hear about the auction, Slow Poke?
Oh yeah, must be a war coming.

Who's fighting?
Ah, that's just an old sponger saying. Sponges are used to clean wounds.
So if someone is buying a lot of them, we say they're getting ready to start a war.
There's an auction coming up real soon. I'm heading out tomorrow. To catch what I can to sell.
You need any help? This fella won't hire me to run his illegal liquor!
I suppose I could use another hand.

Meet me at the docks at dawn.
Sure thing!
My boat's *The Lost Love.*

The Lost Love

The Lost Love
Hey there, honey. You ready to work?
Hi, Slow Poke! You bet I am.
Waves are picking up. You know how to swim, right?
Like a fish.
This is Ollie. He's my new first mate.
Welcome aboard, Miss Turtle.

What happened to the old first mate?
Got bit by a shark.
That happen a lot?!
ha
Only after a few rounds at Sloppy Joe's. The shark was a lovely lady named Margaret.
Hah!
Shark ever bite you?
HAHA
Well...
A long time ago.

SPLASH
Say, you think we'll be attacked anytime soon?
Attacked?
That's what always happens in the comics.
Don't worry, honey.
POMF

Ollie here will beat 'em off.
You bet I will.
HA HA
So where we headed, Captain?
Where do you want to go, honey?
How about...
...China?
China's pretty far away. Might not be home for supper.
I don't mind. I had a big breakfast.
Wait.
You ever been to China for real?

'Fraid not. But I've been to Cuba. And the Bahamas.
Your people are from Green Turtle Key. Mine, too.
Are we related? Seems like everybody here is someone else's cousin.
I don't know, honey.
...
I wish we could go to China for real.

Hey, Ollie, before we start I wanna check on the cistern.
Aye-aye, Cap!
Does anyone live here?
Spongers leave their sponges to cure here sometimes. There's a cistern out back that catches rainwater that we use, too. Want to help me check on it, honey?
YUCK!
This is why we check it.

Hey, what's this?
Hm?
Oh, that... It's a genuine pirate death trap.
Pirates would run a spike through the shackles of their rivals, and let them drown in the incoming tide.
...
You're pulling my leg.
You got me.

But there were pirates around here a long time ago.
I don't believe you.
It's true. See those keys? There's hundreds of them. That's where pirates used to hide their loot.
Everybody's always looking for Black Caesar's treasure. Especially after Old Ropes up and disappeared.
Who's Black Caesar? Who's Old Ropes? And why does every single person in Key West have a weird nickname?
Black Caesar was a ruthless pirate.
Folks say Old Ropes, an old-time sponger, made off with one of Black Caesar's stashes and is living rich as a hog somewhere in South America.

He disappeared one day after having a drink at the bar. Left his house full of furniture, food in the ice box. Even left his cat.
How could he leave his cat?!
Do you think he really found treasure?
I think he found trouble. Old Ropes liked to gamble. I suspect he owed someone money and had to get out of town fast.
Speaking of which, let's go out there and get to sponging!
Aye, Captain!

This water glass will help us better spot sponges.
Oh, I see 'em!
Splash
Sploosh
There's our first sponge!

That's a good day's work. What do you think, Cap?

I see one more!
You want to try for it, Miss Turtle?
All right.
You're a born Conch.
SLIP
WHOA!

SPOOOOOSH
Remember how I said I could swim?
SWIRRRR
Maybe that wasn't entirely accurate.
At least Beans will get his room back...

GASP
THUMP
GEHO
GE–
HACK

You okay, honey?!
Koff
Koff
Yes.
Took ten years off my life!
She went over so fast, Cap.
I thought you said you could swim like a fish.
A dead one...
Sorry.
Honey.
Dead fish float.

A Big, Happy Family

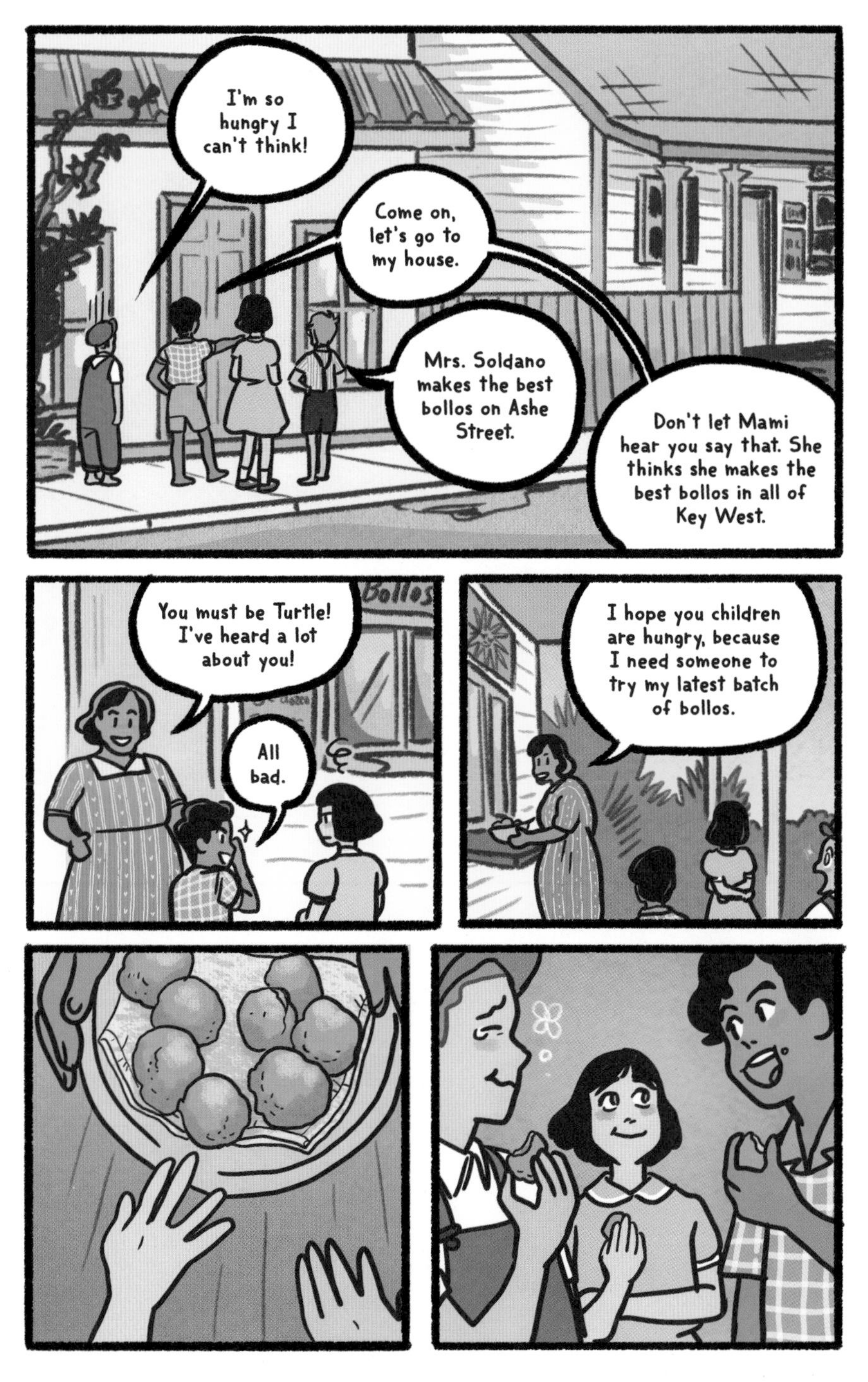
I'm so hungry I can't think!
Come on, let's go to my house.
Mrs. Soldano makes the best bollos on Ashe Street.
Don't let Mami hear you say that. She thinks she makes the best bollos in all of Key West.
Bollos
You must be Turtle! I've heard a lot about you!
All bad.
I hope you children are hungry, because I need someone to try my latest batch of bollos.

These are so delicious.
Kids, take this to Nana Philly.
But, Mami!
Where are we going again?
Bringing Nana Philly her lunch.
Nana Philly is meaner than a scorpion.
Someone lives here?

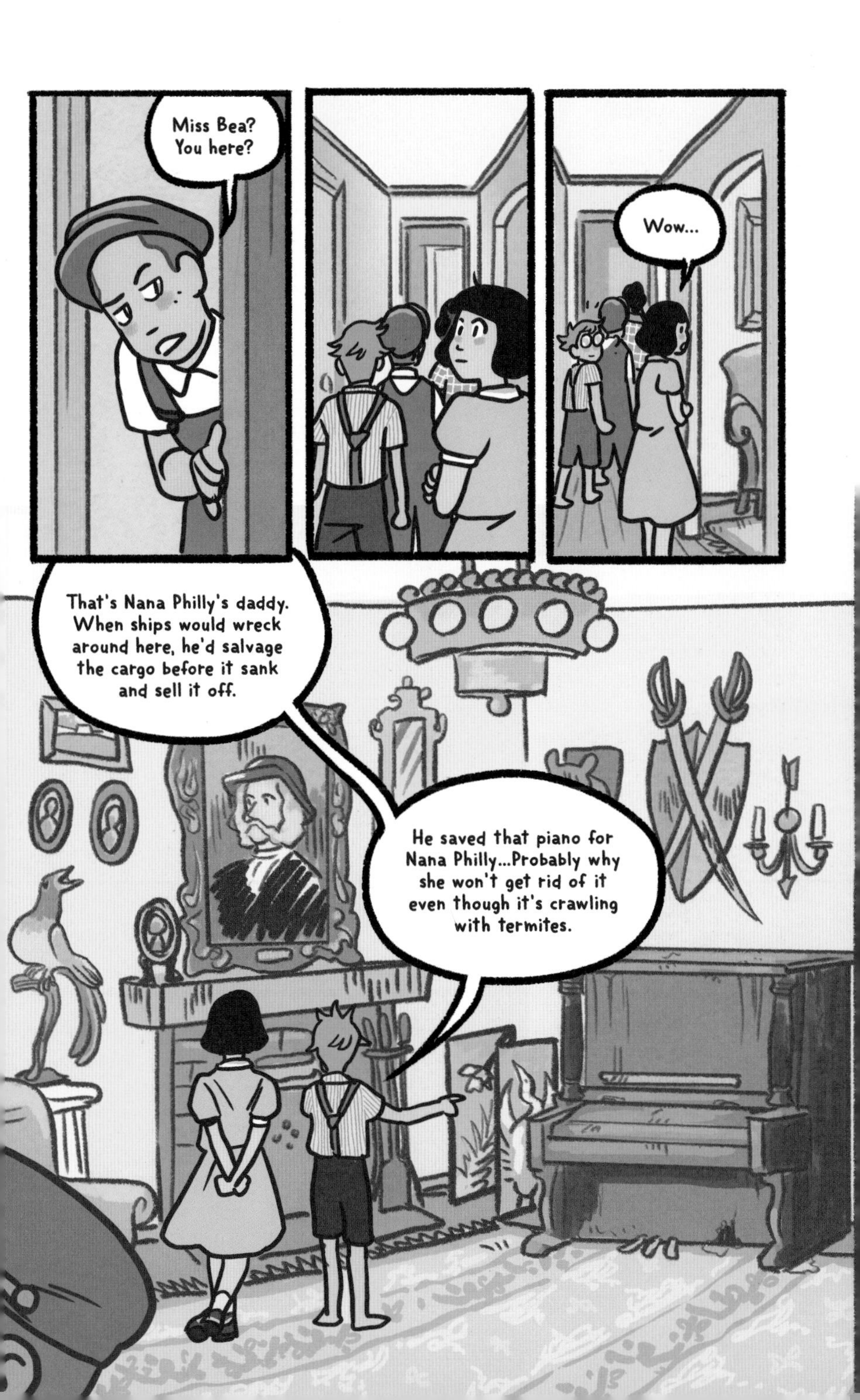
Miss Bea?
You here?
Wow...
That's Nana Philly's daddy. When ships would wreck around here, he'd salvage the cargo before it sank and sell it off.
He saved that piano for Nana Philly...Probably why she won't get rid of it even though it's crawling with termites.

Nana Philly sits in the parlor most days. Miss Bea takes care of her.
Miss Bea!
Hi, Nana Philly.
Thadie?

Hello, children! I was out back hanging laundry. I didn't hear you come in.
Hi, Miss Bea.
Mami's flan for Nana Philly.
How sweet of her! Miss Philomena does love her flan.
You must be Sadiebelle's girl! You look just like your mother. Doesn't she look just like her mother, Miss Philomena?
SMIRK
Eh heh heh...

I don't understand, what's so scary about that old woman? She can barely talk.
I guess you could say she was a little different before she had her accident.
She had a fit last summer and fell and hasn't walked or talked the same since.
Best thing that ever happened, if you ask me.
You said it, pal.
What?! How can you say that about a poor old lady?!
She said Ma would be better off dead than married to Poppy.
She stood up in church and told the minister his sermon was so boring he ought to be crucified!

How can you talk about someone's grandmother like this?
You mean *your* grandmother?
M-my grandmother? But Mama told me she was dead!
She's not dead. She's just mean.
Do I...have a grandfather, too?
Nah, Grampy's dead. Died when Buddy was born.
I can't believe I have a grandmother.
Believe it.
Welcome to the family.

The Diaper Gang Knows

Ira's back!
How was Miami?
Took forever to get home. Eggy's doing better.
What were you doing in Miami?
Who are you?
Oh, I'm just some cousin from New Jersey.

Well, I'm Ira.
My little brother suffers from chronic dumbness and blew his thumb and pinkie off with a firecracker. We had to go to a hospital up there.
So, what'd I miss? Have we had a lot of babies?
We been busy. But we're gonna need a new wagon soon.
Pork Chop. Beans.
Are you boys having a pleasant summer?
Yes, Miss Sugarapple!
Only one reason kids would be that nice.
She your teacher?
Pork Chop and Beans got in big trouble with Miss Sugarapple last year.
They stole the answer sheet for a test from her desk.

They had to stay after school every day for the last month and write "I will not steal" on the chalkboard two hundred times.
We borrowed it!
If I never see her again, I'll be lucky.
HMPH!
Listen to this! I met this kid named Lester in Miami, and he told me about this thing called tick-tocking.
What's that?
All you need is a rock and a string. Miss Sugarapple will never know what hit her.

So it goes like this...
You take a rock and tie it to a long length of string—long enough to reach across a roof.

Then, stake out a house and wait until everyone is asleep.
shhhh
You throw the rock over the house so that it lands on the opposite side near a window.
fling
clack
When you tug on the string, it scrapes the window and makes a scary sound, as if a bony hand is trying to get in the house.
SQUIRRR
AAAAAA AAAA
And you take off running.

AAAAAAA—
WHO'S THERE?!
AAAAA!
Sounds like the Diaper Gang has struck, Smokey.
whip
chirp
That was hilarious, pals! She screamed so loud, I bet they heard her in Cuba!
HA HA HA

Hey, kiddos. Y'all hear about the ghost at Miss Sugarapple's place?
A ghost?
Gee whiz, I sure do hope Miss Sugarapple is okay. She's our favorite teacher.
GRIN
This is the bee's knees, fellas.
GRIN
GRIN

Fliing
WA AAA
clack
AAAAAA
SQUEEEEEK
WAAAAA
AH!
WHO'S THERE?!
GHOST!

WAAAAAAAAAA
WAAAAAAAAA
Pudding... why?
Turtle! Just pick him up already!
WAAAAAAA
I'm not in the Diaper Gang.
Who cares! I'm exhausted. Haunting is hard work.
AAAA
Fellas! You made the paper!
AAA
The Key West
Key West Cursed by Weeping Ghost
Weeping?!
Everyone thinks our ghost is a *crybaby*?

The Man of the House

They might as well have said Pudding is the ghost!
Termite! Leave Smokey alone.
BARK BARK
HISSS
SWIPE
HISS
Come 'ere, Smokes.
Hi there, Miss Turtle.
Hi, Mr. Gardner.
Letter for you.
Sadiebelle Gifford
Turtle
Curry Lane
Key West, Fla.
Thank you.

Dear Turtle,

How are you, baby? I miss you something awful.

Mrs. Budnick never sleeps and doesn't care if anybody else does, either. She thinks nothing of waking me up in the middle of the night to make her tea or toast. I'm so tired I can barely see straight. The only thing that keeps me going is thinking of you.

Someday this will all be behind us, I promise. I've been thinking that maybe I can become an actress. Can't you just see my name in lights? All I need to do now is get a screen test with Warner Brothers.

Love Always,

Mama

Poppy...
Poppy!
Poppy's home!

Hi there, Pork Chop.
Hi, Mr. Curry.
You shaved, Vernon.
Stopped at the barbershop on my way home.
Something you want to tell me?
She's Sadiebelle's girl. Just showed up.
WAAAAAAAAAZZ
That one ours, too?
You haven't been gone that long.

Whenever Archie comes back from a sales trip, it's just like Christmas. He buys treats for me and Mama.
Uncle Vernon doesn't buy treats like Archie, but things are different with him in the house.
He doesn't say much at all.
But I like him.

Gee, I never met a man who could sew.
You know how to sew?
My daddy taught me.
Sure. Housekeeper does the mending.

Not bad.
How are you settling in here?
I'm not used to having cousins.
You'll get used to them. I see you've already acquired a taste for turtle.
What?
Dinner. That was three bowls of turtle soup you had, you know.
I thought it was beef!
Seems mean to eat something you're named after.
Well... nothing mean about filling your belly.

Where'd you get that name of yours?
Mama says I've got a hard shell.
Hard shell, huh? You must take after your aunt. I don't know anyone who's got a harder shell than my Minerva.
You know, the thing about a turtle is that it looks tough, but it's got a soft underbelly.
...
So I hear your mother is seeing a salesman? What's he sell?
Encyclopedias.
He successful?
Archie can sell anything.

Mama really likes him. He's not like all the others.
You know your aunt and your mother were the prettiest girls in Key West in their day.
Mama's still pretty. Mr. Leonard swore he'd leave his wife for her.
The Leonards? Who are they?
A family we worked for. Mrs. Leonard fired Mama. Mama was the third housekeeper Mr. Leonard proposed to.
Now that doesn't seem fair. Sounds like Mrs. Leonard should have fired Mr. Leonard.
You said it. Good help is hard to find.

Ladies Who Lunch

Hey, fellas, got tickets for a matinee.
How'd you get those?
How do you think? Baby had a bad bungy and the formula cleared it right up. His mother was so thankful, reckon she was going to cry.
You ought to patent that formula. You'd be the Rockefeller of diaper rash.
So what's playing?
Some Shirley Temple flick.
Shirley Temple...

I'm sorry, but one of you kids is going to have to go over to Nana Philly's and make her lunch. I've just got too much laundry to do today.
Not me!
Me neither!
No way, no how, Ma!
HUFF
I'll do it... Nana Philly can't be any worse than Shirley Temple.
Thank you, Turtle. You're a good girl.

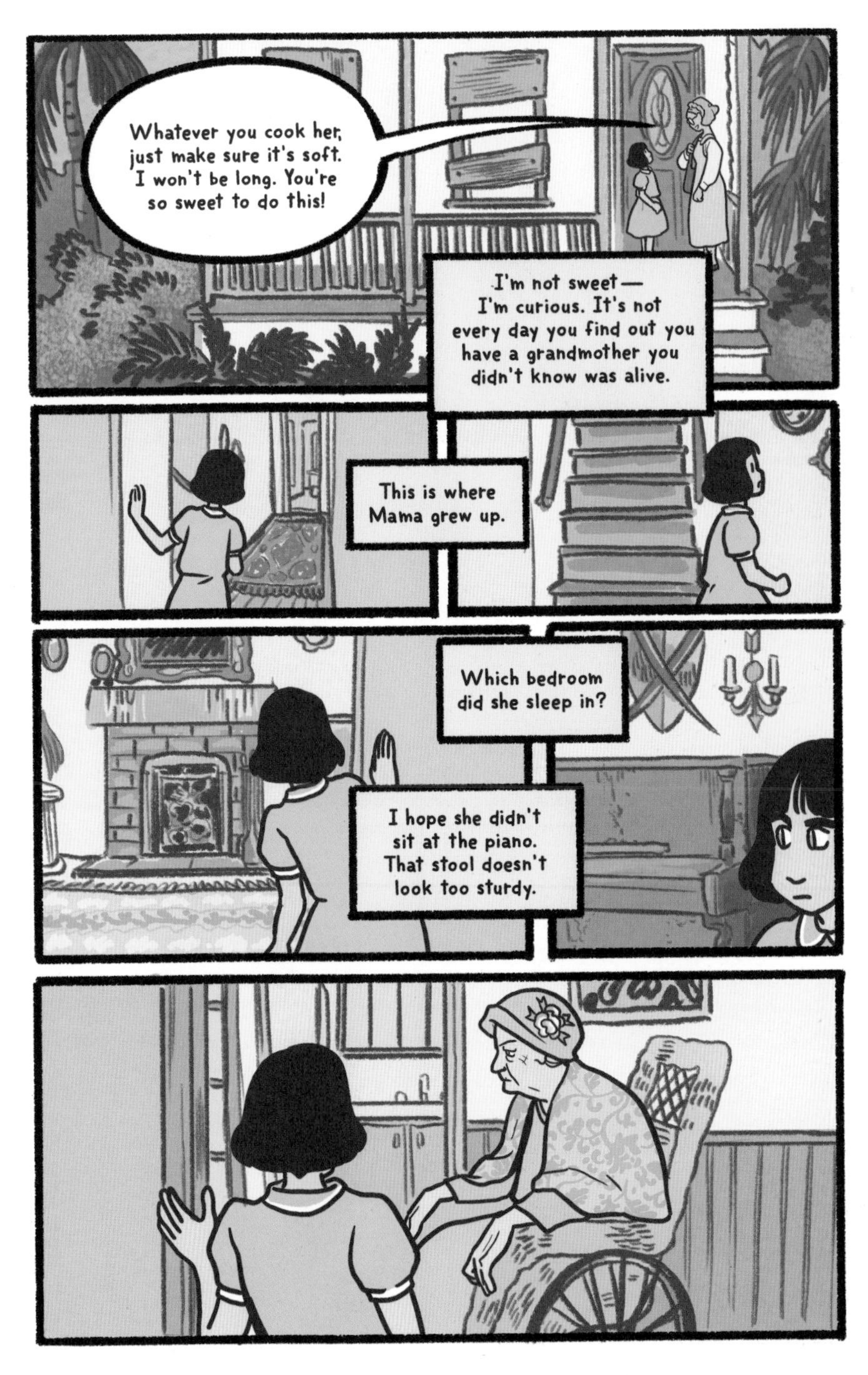
Whatever you cook her, just make sure it's soft. I won't be long. You're so sweet to do this!
I'm not sweet— I'm curious. It's not every day you find out you have a grandmother you didn't know was alive.
This is where Mama grew up.
Which bedroom did she sleep in?
I hope she didn't sit at the piano. That stool doesn't look too sturdy.

I don't know if you remember me, but I'm Turtle. Your granddaughter.
Sadiebelle's girl.
?
Sigh

Just milk and bread, huh?
Bread Box

It's milk toast.
I hope you enjoy it.
...
Oh, no! I forgot your spoon.
CLUNK
What happened?

I must have put it too close to the edge.
Here you go.
SMAK
CLUNK

You did that on purpose! Why? I'm your *granddaughter*.
SMIRK
You don't scare me.
WIPE
SPLASH
SIT

Chomp
This is delicious. Shame you spilled yours.
Chew chew

Did you two have a nice lunch?
We had a lovely time.
Would you like to come again tomorrow? Give your poor aunt a break?
Sure. I'm looking forward to getting to know my grandmother.

hm
hm
Morning, Nana Philly!
Miss Bea made us grits-and-grunts-and-gravy.
clink
PUSH
CRAAASH
Miss Bea sure is a good cook.
Mama's a good cook, too. She makes the best caramel custard.

You know...
Mama told me you were dead.
You were mean to her, weren't you?
Is that why she hasn't come back to Key West?
...
Poor Mama.
RUMBLE

I can tell the old girl's really looking forward to seeing you today.
Even had me get out her best hat.
...
You expecting the queen?
Bubble
Bubble

clink
sluurrp
You know.
I missed seeing a matinee the first day I came to see you... It was a Shirley Temple picture.
Which is fine by me. I hate Shirley Temple.
Me thoo.

Hard Times

The princess needs new shoes.
Thanks, Archie.
GASP!

THMP
THMP
THMP
THMP
THMP
MP
THMP
SWING
Gone...
chirp
chirp
Who do you think took my shoes?
I wouldn't put it past Too Bad.

SLAM
Your cat made a mess in my clean laundry.
Smokey would never do that. She knows better.
That slip's ruined. I'm gonna have to pay Mrs. Felton for that. I'll be lucky if I don't end up owing her more than she owes me.
I swear it wasn't Smokey!
If it happens again the cat's going.

SQUISH
Sigh
Yuck.
Well, if it ain't my favorite deckhand.
Hey, Slow Poke.
So when we going to China? Sooner the better. I sure could stand to find that goldmine. Some kid stole my shoes.

What do you need shoes for, anyhow, Conch kid like you?
To walk in.
Just like your mother, aren't you?
Ha Ha Ha
Believe me, I'm nothing like Mama. I guess you didn't know her very well, huh?
I guess not...
Turtle! Ma's burning mad! She just blew her top.
Smokey ruined Mrs. Felton's skirt! She's in trouble now.

Please, Aunt Minnie, I just know it wasn't Smokey.
She's never done that before and we've lived in a lot of different places. Some other cat must have gotten into the house!
shake
shake

AAAAAAAAAAA!!
WAAAAAA
Sounded like Ma. Do you think someone's tick-tocking us?
GET IT OFF ME!
GET IT OFF ME!

GET IT OFF!
Is Ma going crazy?! Is she gonna start running naked down Duval Street?!
Get what off you, Ma?! I don't see anything!
She is going crazy! She is going crazy!
GET IT OFF ME
Aunt Minnie!
THUMP

Ma!
HISSS
Kermit, look!
Gasp!
HISSSSSS
She's not going crazy, dummy!
She got stung!
Smokey, be careful!
POUNCE

CRUNCH
Did she get it?
Mama's dead...
No, Buddy! She's not dead.
Kermit, fetch a doctor!
I'm going!
TMP
TMP

I've never seen anything like it. She was stung clear down her back. The scorpion was in the nightgown.
She's going to be in a lot of pain. Vomiting. Just keep her comfortable. Where's your father?
He's up in Matecumbe.
Well, if anything changes, you know where to find me. I'll be by again in the morning to check on her.

Sadiebelle?
It's me, Turtle...
I've missed you, Sadiebelle.
...
PAT
Sadiebelle...
I'm back now. I'll take care of you.
Why'd you take my dolls?
Oh, go to sleep already.

Stagger...
Aunt Minnie!
What are you children eating?
Milk toast.
Who cleaned?
Me.
Buddy, have you had any accidents today?
I made him stop playing and use the outhouse.
And I napped a whole hour, Ma!
nod

Smokey killed the scorpion that bit you, Ma! Bit its head right off!
HALT
The cat's still going.

Believing in Monsters

Glad to see me?
Hi there, Turtle.
Miss Philomena has taken a real shine to that cat of yours.
Thanks again for taking her in, Miss Bea.

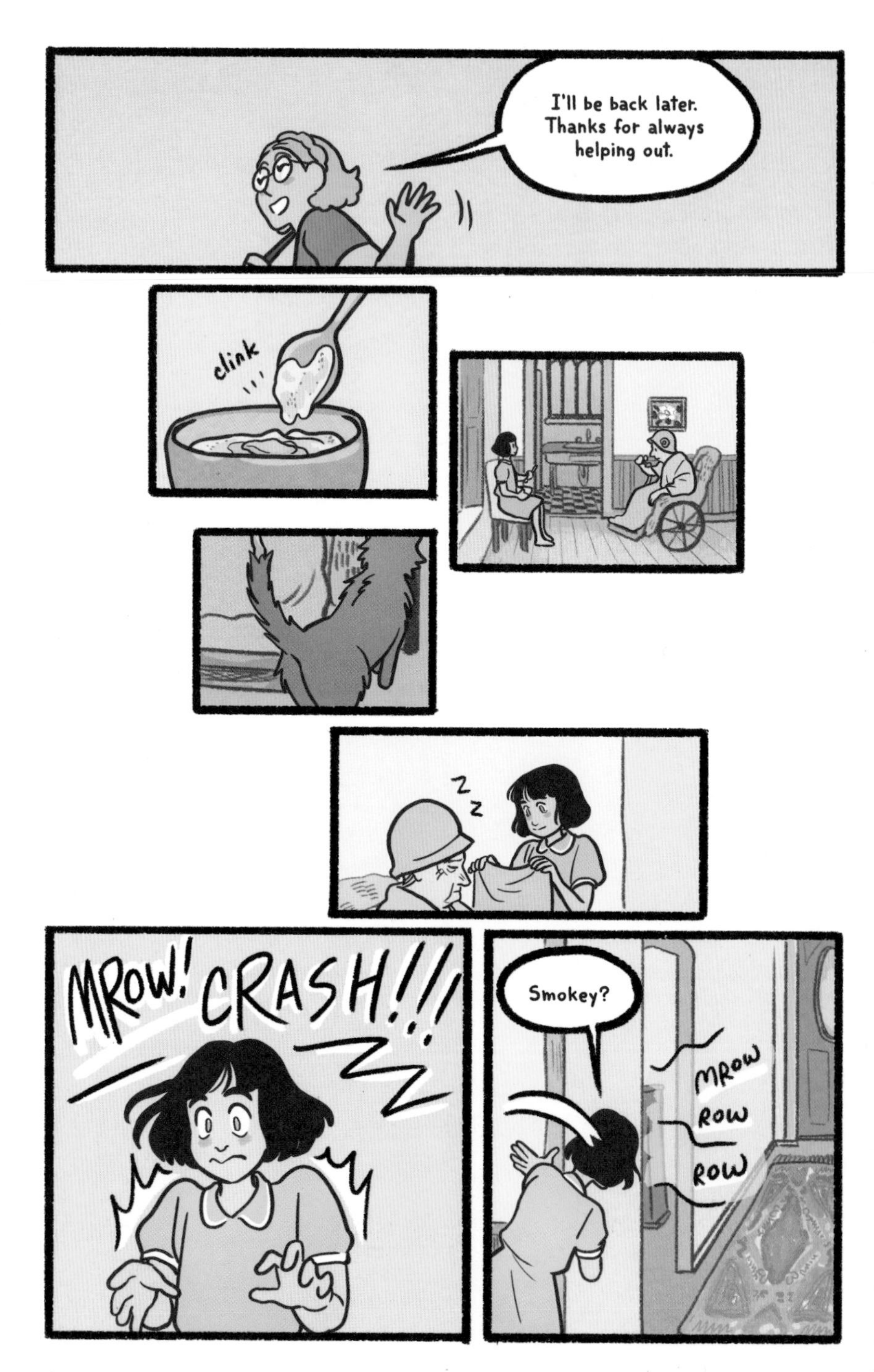
I'll be back later. Thanks for always helping out.
clink
Z
Z
MROW! CRASH!!!
Smokey?
MROW
ROW
ROW

MROW
ROW
scratch
Smokey.
MROW?
Scritch
scratch
Hang on.
Stop moving.
THRASH
WIGGLE
That'll teach you not to jump on furniture.
?
CLUNK
What was that?

peek
In my opinion, the fellas who make Hollywood pictures are really just salesmen. Instead of peddling girdles, they sell chills and thrills.
WIPE
Even comic strips want you to believe an orphan would be adopted by a millionaire.
And perhaps I could believe that.
This being where Blacke Caesar Putte his Treasure
But to believe in this...
!
SNAP
That'd be like believing in bloodsucking vampires and mad scientists bringing dead men to life.

Hey, Turtle.
We're going to challenge those White Street boys to a game of marbles.
If you want to come.
Even as I struggle to believe what I found...
...I keep picturing Mama on her hands and knees scrubbing Mrs. Budnick's floor.
I make a decision.
Wait, fellas!
I think this is a lot more interesting than a marble game.

Lying, Stealing, No-Good Kids

It's a fact:
if a kid is being nice, they're probably up to no good.
We tell Aunt Minnie what Pork Chop and Ira are telling their mothers...
That we're gonna wake up early and go fishing for conch so that we can make conch stew for Labor Day.
Good job getting the boat, Pork Chop.
Rumrunner needs a fast boat.
And we do, too, for treasure hunting!

"Rumrunner needs a fast boat?" Wait a second.
Pork Chop! Is Johnny Cakes letting us use his boat?!
Not exactly.
But he'll never know. He's in Cuba, same as Slow Poke.
You idiot! That's stealing!
We're borrowing it!

I should have worn a hat.
I think it's time for me to be captain.
I don't think so.
Y'all know where you're going, right? We've been out here a while!
We need to go southeast.
We *are* going southeast.
We're going around this key until we see the shack. I know where it is.

Look!
The shack!
Throw in the hook, Pork Chop!
Wait for me!
The map says once we get to the key, we just need to find this tree.
It looks like a "Y."
The trees are gonna be all different. Might not even be around anymore.

Follow me! I got a nose for treasure.
Ugh. I can't dig another hole.
THUNK
I think I'll buy some ice cream with my share of the treasure.
Kermit, you'd better not eat all of Mami's bollos.
Maybe we're just not looking in the right spot.
There is no right spot.

That map's not real. Nana Philly put it there knowing we'd find it.
That doesn't make any sense. She would have mentioned it to somebody a long time ago. Nobody can keep a secret in Key West.
We've been had, fellas!
Let's go, Pork Chop. Maybe we can make it back in time to get some ice cream.
You said it, pal.
They're right... it must be fake. Come on. We better go or they'll leave us here.

Slip
Ah!
You okay, Turtle?
Ow
AHA HA
HA
HA
Look! She fell on her bungy!
HA HA HA
Hah
AAHA HA HA!
My bungy found it!
HA
HA HA
You think the sun's getting to her?

What are you talking about?
That.
So what? It's a "U."
That's a "C"...
For Black Caesar.

A Dream
Come True

CRUNCH
SCOOP
This thing is falling apart.
Hurry up and open it!
What... do we do now?

Whatever we want, pal! We're *rich!* *RICH!*
WA HOO
WHOOP!
HAHA
WAAAAA
YIPPEE!
AHA HA HA
HA HA
WA HOO!
RICH!
How much you think it's worth?
Millions! This is better than winning bolita!
Jingle Jingle
This must be how Little Orphan Annie felt after Daddy Warbucks took her in—
Where's the boat?!

Pork Chop... you didn't throw in the hook.
I did!
I threw it in...
Then what happened to the boat?
I-I- I don't know! Maybe someone came and took it!
Fellas! It'll be okay. Every sponger uses this key. Someone will pick us up.
How fine are we gonna be when Johnny Cakes finds out we lost his boat?
We'll buy him a new boat. We'll buy him a hundred boats! We're rich!
Oh, yeah, I forgot.

We'll divvy this up tomorrow.
We should get some sleep.
The mosquitoes are gonna eat us alive before anyone finds us.

Stop touching me, *Pork Chop.*
I'm not, *Beans!*
This is your fault anyway! If you'd just set the hook!
I *did*! I don't have to take this from you!
I'm leaving!
No, you ain't! I'm leaving first!
Well, at least there's more room now.
Yeah...
Don't worry. We'll get picked up in the morning. Just think about how we're going to spend all this gold.

roll
Guess we can afford a new wagon for the gang.
We could even get two.
What about you, Turtle?
What are you gonna buy?
New shoes.
Shoes? Ha ha. Nobody wears shoes around here.
Who said I was planning to stick around?
...

The Rescue Party

drip
drip
Rain...
SHHHHH
itch
We need to go look for food.
Let's split up.
What if we don't find anything?
SHHHHH
Then we'll starve to death.
SHHHH

Any luck?
CRASH
Not really... Looking for a boat.
Those low clouds. And the sea foam.
Any Conch kid knows what they mean.
It means a storm. A big one.
Haven't you figured out I'm not from around here?

I'm starving.
Maybe we could build a raft?
Out of wood from the shack.
Then we won't have anywhere to sleep!
Who cares about sleeping? Let's just try and get out of here.
We wouldn't be here in the first place if you weren't such a dummy!
I got more sense in my bungy than you've got in your whole body!
Sense?! Even Buddy knows how to set a hook!
I'll show you hook!

WHAM!
Stagger
ERRAAGH!
Come on, fellas, knock it off.
If they kill each other, I get their share of the treasure.
Get off my brother!

I guess I'll try to stop them.
shrug
Fellas, calm down!
STOP
OW! IT
LET GO!
Hey, look! A boat!
What? Where?
It was there just a minute ago.

There's no boat! You lied to make us stop fighting.
You got me. I don't know what I was thinking.
WHOOSH
Patter Patter
SHHHHH
They should just kiss and make up already.
They ever scrap this bad before?
They've been best pals since they were in diapers.

You think anyone's looking for us?
Probably the whole town by now.
SHHHHHH
WHOOSH
CREAK
You think the shack's going to blow away?
I dunno, but Pork Chop and Beans better come inside. I don't want to spend all this gold on a headstone.
I'm not going out there. I've got a weak heart.
Oh. One out of two.

SLUMP
?
You coming in or what?
RUSH
SLUMP

SHHHHHHHHH
KRACKA KOOM!
AH!
SWISH
You think the water's gonna come up any farther?
Wah!! There's a rat in here!

CRACKK
SHHHH
drip
We're all gonna die...
Aw, come on, pal...
We are...
sniff
UUUU
sniff
And it's all my fault...
because I didn't throw the hook in.

THUMP
CRACK
Sniff
SHHHHHHHH
WHOOSH
Sniff
WHSHHHH
Sob
hic
Sniff
SHHHHHHHH
Sniff
THUNK
Sob
WHOOSH
SHHH
hic
Sob
HHH
Sniff

The boys are all bawling like babies. I don't have any blankets to wrap them in or a wagon to soothe them.
For some reason, that dumb Shirley Temple song comes to mind.
On the...
...gooo~od ship...
Lollipop...
It's a
swe~eet trip
to a
candy shop...
RUMBLE
WHOooOSH
SHWOOO

AND THERE YOU
ARE!
HAPPY LANDING ON A CHOCOLATE BAR!
HA HA

A Hollywood Ending

snore

Ma...

CHIIIRPP
CHIIIIRP
Sniff
sniff
Grab

GASP
KIDS!
...
HUFF
CAP! WE FOUND THEM!
Slow Poke!!
TRIP

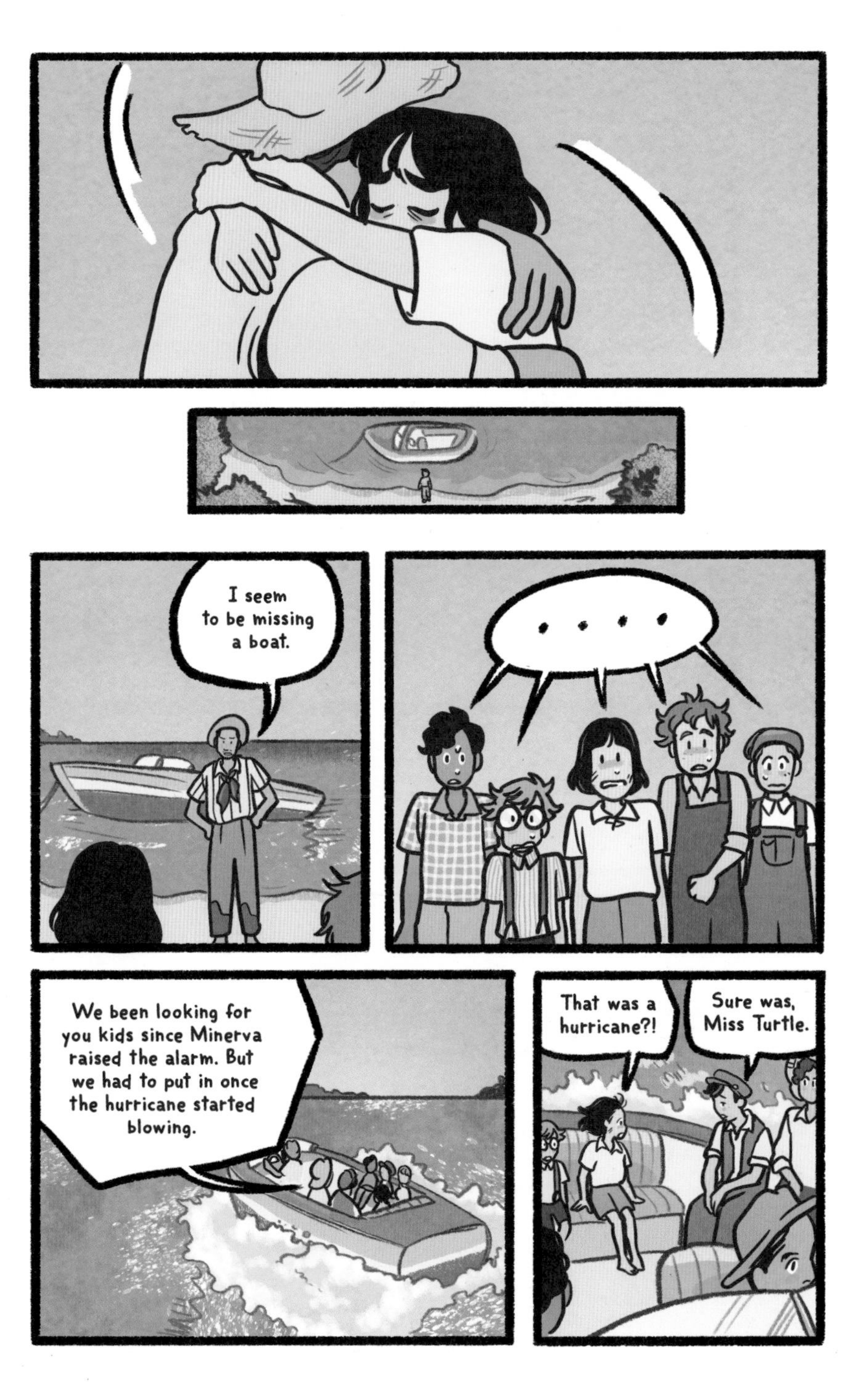
I seem to be missing a boat.
. . . .
We been looking for you kids since Minerva raised the alarm. But we had to put in once the hurricane started blowing.
That was a hurricane?!
Sure was, Miss Turtle.

Key West came through it all right. But word is, upper keys got hit hard.
Poppy!
He's fine, Kermit. He wasn't even there when it hit. Came down when he heard y'all were missing. You saved his life.
How'd you figure out where we went?
That kid who's always tagging around after you.
TOO BAD?!
We were saved by Too Bad? Aw, we're never gonna live this down, fellas.
What were you kids even thinking?
We were thinking about this!
!

We split the treasure money with Nana.
Aunt Minnie had us kids put our portions in the bank.
Although, we did buy a few things.
The Key West
STILL TAKING TOLL
GANG OF CHARMING KIDS FINDS PIRATE TREASURE LOOT OF $20,000!
Why'd they say gang? It's Diaper Gang. Two words.
My eyes are closed! Why'd they print that photo?
Charming? Guess they never met you.

Well, if it ain't the Diaper Gang. That a new wagon?
It sure is, Jelly!
Got a new member in your little gang, I see.
That's right! I'm in the Diaper Gang now! I saved their lives!
And guess what! I know the secret formula! It's cornstarch—
Too Bad! First rule of the Diaper Gang is "Shut UP, already!"
HA HA

...Mama?
Mama!
Baby.
I missed you, Mama.

Miss me, too, princess?
Archie!
You can call me Daddy now.
You got married?!
Oh, Mama!
Sadiebelle.

It's been a long time.
Slow Poke...
Slow Poke's the one that rescued us!
He is?
In that case, I owe you a debt, sir.
For looking after our little girl here.
Archie Meeks.
Pleased to meet you.

Huh, too late again.
What a funny fella, and what kind of a name is Slow Poke?
What did he mean, "again"?
Nothing, I'm sure.

Paradise Found

Good night, baby. We'll just be in the room next door.
Archie sure did find the nicest hotel in Key West, huh?
He sure did, baby.
This is probably the nicest bed I've ever slept in.
Get some sleep. I'll see you at breakfast.
click

I'll check out of the hotel and arrange to get the luggage over to the docks. I'll meet you at your sister's place at noon.
That should leave plenty of time to say your goodbyes and for us to make our boat.
Don't forget to stop at the bank, Mr. Meeks.
KISS
As if I would forget, Mrs. Meeks.
Isn't this like a dream come true? I feel like Cinderella!
She scrubbed floors, too.

No more scrubbing floors for me! You should have seen Mrs. Budnick's face when I quit, baby!
Now me, you, and Archie are gonna get us a lovely plot of land in Georgia. A perfect place for the Bellewood.
Mama, can I ask you something?
Of course, baby.
How well did you know Slow Poke?
...

Not very well at all, as it turned out...
He's...
my—
Enough about that!
We better hurry along and say goodbye to Minnie.
I wish we'd been able to stay for a longer visit, but Archie is anxious to start our new life together.
I want to say goodbye to Smokey. She's at Nana Philly's house... You should see her before we go.
Oh...
Turtle, uhm...
I don't know if I can face her.
She said I wasn't her daughter anymore...She said I was a disgrace.
SLUMP
Oh, Mama... I'm sure that's not the meanest thing she's ever said.

Nana Philly? I've come to say goodbye.
We're going to Georgia...
Nice hat... Did you buy that with your cut of the treasure?
mrow
Take care of Smokey for me.
You know, Aunt Minnie said while we were stuck on the key, a stray cat got in and made a mess in the laundry.
I guess Aunt Minnie will learn to listen to me now.
...
sigh
I'm gonna miss our lunches.
Me thoo...

There's someone else who wants to say goodbye.
Mother...

Sniff

You have to visit, okay, Turtle? I wanna play marbles!
Don't give her any ideas. I just got my room back.
Hey, fellas!
Oh, Turtle. What are you doing here?
I'm not gonna miss you, either.
No, I mean... what are you doing here? I saw your new daddy leave.
What?

Dark hair?
Panama hat?
I saw him get on a boat hours ago.
Boat was going to Cuba, though. Thought that was strange.
HURK
Are you gonna puke, Turtle?
Archie can sell anything.
gasp
And it turns out I'm as much of a sucker as anybody.
He sold me a dream...
Mama happy, a home, a family at last...
And I bought it hook, line, and sinker.

Mama...
What is it, baby? Archie outside?
No, Mama...
Archie's not coming...
What?
Oh, Sadiebelle...

What? I don't understand. Did something happen to him?
He's gone, Mama.
Archie's dead?!
Well...Mami always says that Cuba is her idea of heaven.
Cuba? What are you talking about?
Aunt Sadie! Archie took Turtle's part of the treasure and hopped on a boat to Cuba!

No.
Please, Mama...
I don't believe you!
Mama!

Mama!
Mama! Stop!
!
SOB

SOB
HIC
sniff
But he promised!
He promised he'd take care of us!
UUUUUAAH-- hic
AAAA
SOB
AAAA
It's okay, Mama.
Everything'll be fine...
Uncle Vernon was right—I do have a soft underbelly.
It's Mama.
AH-HUH
SOB
SNIFF

WIPE
SNIFF
Turtle!
BUMP

Uh, say, you want to be in the Diaper Gang?
hah
I don't like babies.
What about paper dolls?
I have some nice ones.
They belong to the family... So you're going to have to stay here if you want to play with them.
Your mother, too.

Aw, just say you'll stay, Turtle.
All right.

Besides, you already got a dumb nickname like everyone else around here.
Beans!
HA HA HA
I've lived long enough to learn the truth:

Not all kids are rotten...
...and there are grown-ups who are sweet as Necco Wafers.
And if you're lucky, some of them may even end up being your family.
The End

Acknowledgments

Warm thanks for everyone who helped Turtle find her way home, especially the Key West Art and Historical Society, Kurt and Monica Lewin, Michelle Nagler, Gina Gagliano, and Lark Pien.

–J.H.

Thank you to the supportive team at Random House Graphic, Lark Pien, my friends, and my wonderful partner, Stephen.

–S.G.

About the Authors

Jennifer L. Holm's great-grandmother emigrated from the Bahamas to Key West in 1897. She has written two Key West novels: *Turtle in Paradise* and *Full of Beans*, which won the Scott O'Dell Award for Historical Fiction. She is a *New York Times* bestselling author and the recipient of three Newbery Honors for her novels *Turtle in Paradise, Our Only May Amelia,* and *Penny from Heaven.* She is also the author of other highly praised books, including *The Fourteenth Goldfish* and *The Third Mushroom.* With her brother Matthew Holm, she is the co-creator of the Eisner Award-winning Babymouse series, the Squish series, and the Sunny Side Up graphic novels.

Savanna Ganucheau is a comic artist from New Orleans. She co-authored her first graphic novel, *Bloom*, in 2019 with Kevin Panetta. *Bloom* received a distinction from the Junior Library Guild and a GLAAD award nomination, and was Amazon's pick for Best Graphic Novel of the Year. Savanna has been creating comics since she was in third grade, and she self-published her work in local comic book shops throughout high school. Savanna has also contributed to such comic series as Adventure Time, Lumberjanes, Jem and the Holograms, and The Backstagers.

Lark Pien is the colorist of *American Born Chinese, Boxers and Saints, Dragon Hoops, Stargazing, Sunny Side Up, Swing It, Sunny,* and *Sunny Rolls the Dice.* She has authored three picture books and is the creator of the Long Tail Kitty series and *Mr. Elephanter.* Lark began making mini-comics in 1997 and is making them still today. You can find occasional tweets and IG posts at @larkpien.

A Note from Jennifer L. Holm

Turtle in Paradise was inspired by my Conch great-grandmother, Jennie Lewin Peck, who emigrated with her family from the Bahamas to Key West in the late 1800s. As a child, I heard about Spanish limes and sugar apple ice cream and the importance of shaking out your shoes to avoid scorpions. My family is related to the Curry family of Key West, after whom Curry Lane is named.

Many families suffered hardship during the Great Depression, and it was not unusual for parents to leave home in search of work or for children to be cared for by relatives. Then, as now, entertainment was a great distraction, and movies, radio shows, and the funny pages provided much amusement for everyone. Little Orphan Annie, Shirley Temple, and the Shadow were all superstars in their day.

Shirley Temple popping through a 1935 calendar

At the height of the Depression, Key West was in economic ruin, with the majority of the population on public relief. The town officially declared bankruptcy. FERA, the Federal Emergency Relief Administration, came into Key West in 1934 with the intent of reinvigorating the economy by marketing it as a tourist attraction. Key West was on its way to recovery when what became known as the Labor Day Hurricane struck on September 2, 1935. While the Lower Keys and Key West were largely spared, the Middle and Upper Keys bore the brunt of the storm, with terrible loss of life.

Searching for pirate loot has always been a popular pastime in the Keys. Jeane Porter, in her book *Key West: Conch Smiles*, writes, "When I was a little girl in the early '30s everybody in Key West had a treasure story." While actually finding pirate treasure may seem far-fetched, historical rumors abound. In Charlotte Niedhauk's account of living in the Florida Keys during this time, *Charlotte's Story*, she relates the tale circulating around Key West of a sponge fisherman who mysteriously disappeared with his family to South America after finding the treasure of a pirate named Black Caesar. Whether Black Caesar ever visited the Keys is still a matter of speculation.

Pepe's Café is a beloved institution in Key West. It still exists, although it is no longer on Duval Street.

Pepe's Café, Key West, Florida, circa 1938

Key West children posing on the docks with five turtles and a pile of sponges in the background

The sponging industry and turtle kraals are remnants of the past, but they were once thriving industries. Nicknaming was a Key West tradition, and the nicknames came in all styles. The scorpion sting suffered by Aunt Minnie was inspired by an actual incident.

Likewise, some of the characters had their inspiration in actual people. The writer Ernest Hemingway was one of Key West's most famous residents. He was in Key West when the Labor Day Hurricane struck, and he witnessed the aftermath firsthand and wrote about it. In true Key West fashion, he had a nickname among the locals—Papa. Kermit was inspired by my cousin Kermit Lewin. The real Kermit suffered rheumatic fever as a child and grew up to become the mayor of Key West in the 1960s. He famously tricked Jimmy the ice cream man with the "nickel in the bottom of the cup" trick to get free ice cream, and he did tick-tock people. Killie the Horse and Jimmy were actual local characters of Key West.

The real Kermit (left) circa 1930, with the family friend who inspired Pork Chop

Finally, the Diaper Gang's secret diaper-rash formula is a family remedy I have used on my own babies' bungys. (It also works on mosquito bites.)

My family's recollections, and those of many other Conchs, provided the details of everyday life in this book, and I am grateful to them all for sharing their memories.

Jenni

A typical Conch neighborhood in Key West, circa 1935

A Note from Savanna Ganucheau

Historical fiction was my favorite genre throughout middle school, and I know that a Turtle-aged Savanna would have loved to read *Turtle in Paradise.*

When starting this project, the biggest challenge was truly appreciating a place that I have never been to, and imagining what it was like well before I was born. Much of my time was spent looking up specific details with little photographic evidence, like the exact species of sponge they used to harvest in Key West. It is hard to express the excitement I felt when I finally found a map of 1930s Key West and began to piece together Turtle's exact steps through the town. This book was a crash course in visually researching a historical location.

Many of the visuals and experiences in Key West really spoke to me. When I was Turtle's age, I lived in a small beach town in Mississippi, and I dreamed of an adventure just like hers. The neighbors called me the marine biologist because I was always on the beach, investigating creatures that would wash up on shore at the end of their life in the gulf. Turtle is similarly curious, and I know I would have connected with her when I was younger.

The development of *Turtle in Paradise* was quick and intense, and I've read so much about Key West that it truly feels like I've been there. From the history of the Bahama Village to struggling through historical boat research, I've learned about Key West through many lenses. I can only hope I did the Conchs' unique town justice.

To the readers, I hope that you enjoyed this book and that your mind, like Turtle's, stays curious and questioning.

Making the Art of *Turtle in Paradise* with Savanna Ganucheau

Here's how a page of *Turtle in Paradise* came together from start to finish! Everyone's process is different, but this is how I work on comic pages.

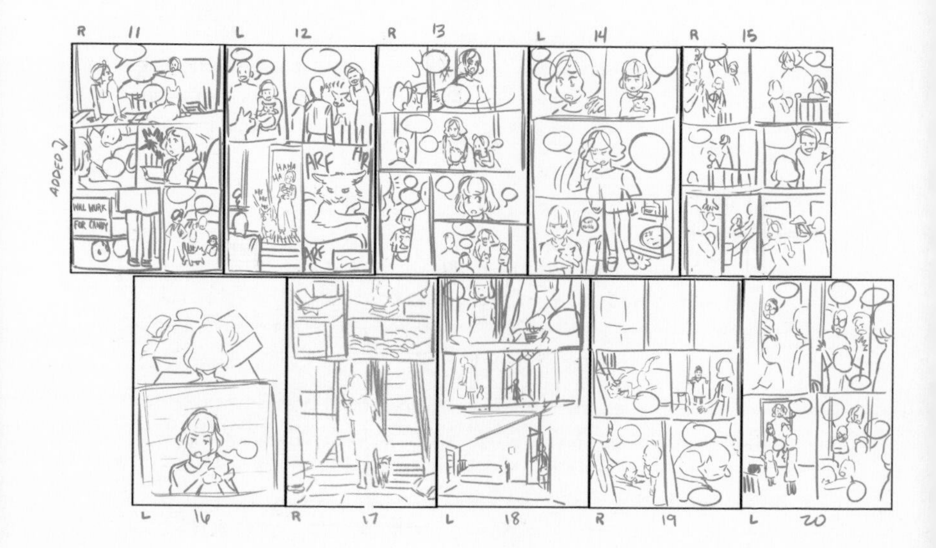

Step 1: Thumbnails

After the script is finished, I work on thumbnails. This is when I figure out where the panels and characters will go on the page. This step is very helpful to see if the page works well with the surrounding pages.

Step 2: Pencils

The next step is to finalize the layout and sketch the figures and backgrounds. In this example, you can see how I changed things to show more of the house and added a reaction shot of Turtle entering.

Step 3: Inks

The inks step is where everything gets polished. During this step, the lettering is also finalized.

Step 4: Colors

After I finish inks and everything is approved by the editor, I hand the page over to the colorist, Lark!

From Lark
Turtle and company were colored in Photoshop, with a few Kyle T. Webster brushes. I like to color scene by scene, rather than page by page!

Concept Art

My first-ever drawing of Turtle and Smokey, accompanied by the foliage of a Key West lane.

Here are the initial concepts for the Diaper Gang and the grown-ups. Turtle has a bit more personality here than above. For the grown-ups, it was interesting to focus on a family resemblance between Sadie and Minnie, while incorporating some of their features in Turtle's face as well.

Turtle in Paradise
THE DIAPER G

Turtle Beans Pork chop kermit Ira Buddy

Nana Philly

with hat

Nana Philly was the last character I designed. It was important to me that she resembles the rest of the Giffords, while also conveying a stern appearance.

Early Cover Concepts

Turtle in
Paradise